Nana's SECRET Christmas Room

Nana's SECRET Christmas Room

MICHELE MORAN

ISBN: 978-1-965679-27-2 (sc)
ISBN: 978-1-965679-28-9 (e)

Rev. date: 10/15/2024

TABLE OF CONTENTS

CHAPTER 1

The Move

In the fall of 1956, the world was quite peaceful. Often, the highlight of the day for most families was time spent in front of America's newest friend – a flickering black and white television set that brought us hours of mindless joy watching "I Love Lucy" or "Bonanza". Dining rooms were abandoned, as families invested in folding TV trays set up in front of the television set. The meals eaten there were called "TV dinners"; foil-wrapped trays with three compartments, usually one of chewy Salisbury steak, complemented by whipped potatoes and a small section of baked sliced apples. There were no major wars then, and no giant towers falling in front of our eyes. Life was quite good for most families, and "Father Knows Best" was far more than a comforting television show; it was reality.

In the midst of this peaceful order, my family decided to move from sun-drenched California to the chilly Northwest, to a small farming community near Bend, Oregon. As a ten-year-old boy, I was not a happy camper. I felt like my parents were asking me to leave behind all my best friends, neighborhood baseball games, and year-round warm temperatures in trade for strange "Oregonian" children, who I felt might not even know how to play baseball. I also pictured icy cold, long and dreary stretches of winter.

We were moving because, as Mom had calmly explained to me, my dad had lost his construction job. He couldn't find another that paid enough to care of me, mom, and my baby sisters Olivia and Isabelle, 2-year-old twins. The reason we decided to head north, she continued, was that my Grandpa had recently passed away and left Grandma, or "Nana", as she liked to be called, with an old family lumber mill deep in the Oregon woods. Grandpa nurtured the mill for nearly 40 years. However, Nana found it difficult to care for things alone, and manage the small crew who worked there. So, Dad planned to learn the business and take it over, at least for a year or two. This was until the mill was on its feet. By then, Dad figured, he could find work back home in California.

It seemed to me that my mom was as unhappy about the move

north as I was. But, she was totally devoted to Dad, so she calmly packed our things, filled several brightly colored tins with dozens of home-baked cookies, and off we drove, away from our cozy neighborhood, church, friends, and the only home I had ever known.

So, there we were in our cramped "woody" station wagon, driving north on the new highways, followed by a large yellow moving van carrying our furniture and small personal treasures.

Even my Nana in Oregon was an "unknown" to me. Faint memories of the two visits she and Grandpa made to California, plus a few old photographs had me picturing her as short and slightly plump, with silvery hair swept into a "bun" on the top of her head. She had a very wide smile in every picture that gave her face a jolly appearance. Nana had always remembered my birthdays by sending cheery cards and never failed to tuck few dollar bills inside.

Our plan was to stay with her for a few days when we first arrived in Oregon, and gradually move into our own home, about a quarter-mile down the road. Mom explained it would be a log cabin on the mill property; an old caretakers' house Nana recently cleaned and updated for our trip north. Mom said the cabin was right on a creek, a fact that sounded interesting and raised the possibility of fishing and wading. So, I tried to stay hopeful and pictured lots of kids my age living close by.

We drove for what seemed like endless hours, and as we got

closer to Oregon, there was a chill in the air. I watched orange leaves fall from a few hearty maple trees along the roadside and swirl into tiny tornadoes on the road ahead of us. The rolling hills that towered around us were thick with thousands of pine trees that seemed to sway together in slow motion in the strong wind. Heading further into what can only be called a dark emerald green forest, my eyes grew heavy. I drifted to sleep thinking of Deano, my golden retriever, who had to temporarily be left behind with my Aunt Carol. The plan was that he would stay there until we were settled in and Mom and Dad decided we were ready for a large dog at the cabin. I managed to blink away a few hot tears as I thought about Deano, and hoped he would be sent up to us soon. He was my best friend.

CHAPTER 2

Nana's House

I'm not sure how long I slept, but when my eyes blinked open, it was pitch dark as the car bumped along a dirt road. "Jim!" My Mom was almost shouting at my Dad. "I think I see her porch lights ahead," and as my Dad negotiated some major potholes, sure enough - up ahead we all saw an old white house, complete with cheerful lights shining in the windows through lacy drapes. In addition, there was a silvery head peeking out through the etched oval glass of a large oak door.

"It's Nana's house!" I found myself shouting, so anxious to get out of the car and stretch my legs. I was also very hungry and thought a jelly sandwich sounded good.

"Not so fast," my dad said as I piled out of the back seat. "Help mom with your sisters, then come back and get your suitcase."

I moaned but did as dad said. As I stepped out of the cramped back seat, I got my first good look at Nana's house. It looked very old - Mom called it "Victorian". It was nearly three stories high, and complete with what she said was a "turret" – a round room with a round pointed roof on top, on a corner of the third floor. I remember thinking it reminded me of a castle. I put exploration of its' nooks and crannies on my list of things to do.

After it seemed that Mom had a good grip on my sleeping sisters, I dragged my own small wicker suitcase up to the covered porch that went all around the front of the cozy-looking house. An old wooden swing that would hold at least three people hung invitingly by the front door next to giant clay flowerpots that held the remains of some droopy late-fall petunias.

I was greeted by a warm hug from Nana.

"Little Jeremy," she said lovingly and warmly as she looked at me. "You are so tall and so *handsome.*"

I tried to smile, but my face drooped instead as exhaustion took over. "Poor things," she cooed as she hugged me again and reached over to grab one of my sisters out of my mom's arms. "Audrey, you must all be so tired. Just head up to your rooms and you can unpack and see the house tomorrow."

"Sounds awfully good." Dad exclaimed as he headed into the house and up a winding staircase, dragging our heavy, well-worn suitcases behind him.

"Irene (my Nana's other name)," Mom said softly. "We can't thank you enough for what you are doing. These are tough times for Jim, and you letting us use the cabin is something we appreciate beyond words."

"Nonsense!" Nana harrumphed. "You are my family and would do the same for me. And I know Jim will do a great job with the mill. Besides, it's been so lonely here since ..." she paused. I figured she was thinking of my Grandpa and missing him. "Anyway," she went on with a deep sigh, looking down at me. "I'll bet *someone* could use a bite to eat before bed. How about a glass of milk and a jelly sandwich?" she asked, holding my chin in her soft hands and looking right into my eyes.

I wondered then and many times after that if Nana could somehow read my mind. But no matter. Of course I said yes, and she was off to her kitchen and returned in what seemed like moments carrying a sandwich thick with strawberry jam oozing out of the sides. A peanut butter cookie and a glass of creamy-tasting milk accompanied the treat, and I murmured a shy, "Thank you," then headed upstairs to explore the new surroundings and see where I would sleep for the night.

To my delight, I had a small room all to myself, complete with a soft feather bed and strategically placed piles of Donald Duck comic books at eye level in the tiny closet. Once again, Nana seemed to know me very well. I slipped into my green flannel pajamas, went down the hall for a kiss and prayers with mom and dad, then snuggled in the chilly sheets and started to read. I soon drifted off, however, before finding out if Donald was trumped by Huey, Duey, and Louie.

I woke up the next morning to the smell of sizzling bacon and the soft sounds of someone humming familiar tunes. Creeping down the steps, I saw Nana skittering energetically around the kitchen as she turned the bacon, flipped four large pancakes on the top of an old cast iron cook-stove, and set out a pitcher of fresh, pulpy orange juice and another of cold, creamy milk covered with moisture-beads on its' side as it met the warm air of the kitchen.

"Well, good morning Mr. Jeremy!" she said cheerily as she patted my head, kissed my nose, and bustled past me to begin cracking brown eggs into a buttery iron fry pan. "I hope I didn't wake you up, I'm afraid I'm very noisy when I cook," she went on.

"No Nana – I just smelled the bacon," I said truthfully, walking around the blue and white kitchen, taking note of the dozens of flowered teacups on her shelves, and the incredible smells coming from inside the stove.

She must have followed my gaze and said, "Come here and

see what Nana's got cooking for you all," as she opened the warm door with brightly flowered hot pads on her small hands. I felt like I could float on the smell of the bubbling cinnamon rolls as she slowly took them out of the oven and sat them on the table. "I know this is a lot of food," she said almost apologetically, "but I want to send some down to the cabin with you today so your mama doesn't have to cook much, until the unpacking and moving is done." She went on to say that the crew of the moving truck that had come with us last night had worked very late, stacking our furniture in the cabin. I had the feeling Nana had stayed up late, too, and had been at the cabin with them to oversee the project and be sure it was done right.

"Nana," I began, with more confidence this time, as I could see she was clearly not the cranky type of grandma some kids had. "Why does the milk look so ... thick and so creamy?"

She laughed. "Jeremy, I guess you never had milk right from a cow, have you?" Right from a cow? She has a cow? Things were looking up.

"Nana, can you show her to me after breakfast, please?" I asked hopefully.

"Well, we need to check with your folks first. I imagine they can use some help putting things away and all. "Oh, good morning Audrey, good morning Jim," she interjected as the rest of the family swept into the cheery kitchen, the girls squealing, "We are hungry mama, we are hungry."

Dad led a simple prayer, thanking God for our safe trip. Then we all ate heartily, drastically reducing the possibility of leftovers. Mom, Dad and Nana decided to sit and chat for a few minutes as she served some very black coffee while my sisters played with pots and pans from her cupboards, as they crawled across the warm wooden floor.

Since everyone seemed occupied, I quietly slipped away to explore a little. I decided first to find out what was behind a tall, narrow door, near the far corner of the room, by the hallway. I had been studying the door during breakfast and noticed that it went all the way to the ceiling. It was painted a very light blue, like the rest of the kitchen, and had an old-fashioned glass doorknob. I turned it slowly, quietly pulled the door open and slipped inside to find myself in a long, narrow pantry. It was colder than the rest of the house, and the walls were lined with what seemed to be hundreds of jars of canned fruit and vegetables. Beans, tomatoes, peaches, and some fruits I didn't even recognize peered down at me in the dim room. Large bags of flour and sugar were also stacked on the sagging wooden shelves along with spices I couldn't name, but whose smells were familiar and filled the room with exotic aromas. Tall metal tins labeled "coffee" and "tea" were there as well, and there were three covered bowls of real butter lining a shelf on the outside wall, where it was coldest.

"I see you found my pantry," Nana's voice said behind me. I was startled and looked guilty.

"Jeremy, you can go into any room in my house if you want to," she said, smiling. "But there is not much in here to see that would interest a little boy," she went on, as she gently ushered me out the narrow door. I wasn't so sure. There was more I wanted to see. At the end of the long rows of shelves, behind some brooms and mops and an old wooden bucket, I was sure I had seen another door, another glass doorknob and I wanted to explore. Well, another time.

The rest of the day was spent driving back and forth over the bumpy road from Nana's house to our "new" log home as we began to move in.

CHAPTER 3

Getting to Know You

I liked the cabin. It was old and a little rugged, but very cozy. My mom and Dad were grateful for the work Nana had done before we arrived that included adding some new kitchen cupboards, sprucing up the two small bathrooms, and a good chimney cleaning so we could use the old river-rock fireplace that filled one entire wall of the living room.

"Jeremy, this will be your chance to learn to cut firewood, and help keep the wood bin full," Dad said, as though it were an honor. I sighed. Another adjustment to the country; heating an entire house with chopped wood!

As the unpacking went on over the next few days, we reached the point of leaving Nana's and spent the first night as a family in our cabin. Drifting to sleep, I could hear the wind in the pines and the murmur of the small creek that flowed behind the cabin.

I also thought I heard Mom and Dad down the hall talking about taking me to my new school the next day to meet my teacher and classmates. I guess I should have been excited, but I missed my old friends from California very much, but especially my dog Deano. Two-year-old baby sisters weren't much fun for a 10-year-old boy, and our house didn't seem to be "next door" to anyone else. But, Nana said she thought a neighbor about a half-mile down the road might have kids around my age, so I was hopeful.

School in the country seemed strange to me. The desks had wooden tops that lifted-up with trays for pens and pencils on top. The black iron legs were bolted to the floors of the drafty old building. This fourth-grade classroom also held third grade students, because there were so few rooms in the red clapboard building. Each of the four classrooms had to accommodate two grades, so the teacher worked quickly between the two groups, giving assignments and correcting papers. After a few days, I decided she was a "nice lady" but making friends with the other kids was hard. I could tell they had been friends with each other for years, and they kept talking about their good times together on the family farm in the area, picking fruit in the summer. There were also stories of winter sledding parties on nearby hills, and ice skating on "Miller's Pond" in winters past.

As the days went by, things got a little better as my days fell into a routine of meeting the school bus each morning, taking the long ride home in the afternoon, and chopping wood before I did my homework. Mom was getting used to her new kitchen and began to cook some of my old favorite dinners. Dad started his training at the mill and seemed to be enjoying the new challenge. I finally made it down to the creek one Saturday morning. Although the weather was getting colder as November approached, I could see the potential for wading and fishing when spring and summer came around. For now, the frogs had hibernated, and I could only use my imagination. I pictured picnics by the creek in the summer and hoped to be able to bring new friends over, maybe building dams and even a treehouse in a large maple tree that hung over the creek.

But, since close friendships with the other kids hadn't yet happened, I just rode my bike up to Nana's a few days each week for a visit, taking treats she and my mom cooked for each other and sent back and forth in a wicker basket hung on my handlebars.

One chilly day late in October, Nana took me out to the small red barn behind her house where the old cow, Nestle, would chew her cud while Nana gently milked her dry twice each day. I was a little leery at first, but eventually felt comfortable with the gentle black and white beast, and soon proudly filled my first tin bucket with milk. I watched as Nana took it up to her kitchen where she chilled it in glass bottles, and later skimmed thick, golden cream from the tops. She explained that she used this to make the butter I had seen in the dishes in the pantry. I watched as she used some of that same cream, whipping it by hand to make a yummy topping for the tart cherry pie she baked.

Later that day, as we sat together in her warm kitchen (after I had eaten an exceptionally large piece of pie), Nana said "Jeremy, you seem a little quiet. Is everything all right?" I hesitated. I really didn't want her to worry or to say anything to mom, who had enough to keep her busy, managing my 2-year-old fireball sisters and still getting settled into the new house. Again, as if she had read my mind, she said "Jeremy, when you talk to me, it stays between you and me. I would only say something to your folks if I thought you were in some kind of danger. Does that help?"

I took a deep breath. "Nana, it's just that … well … I guess I feel kind of …" My words trailed off.

"Kind of lonely for your friends, and maybe a little sad sometimes?" she said, making it easier for me.

"Yes Nana. I just wish … I guess I wish it was warmer and that I had my old friends and my dog Deano and that the kids at school liked me more." I blurted out all at once, realizing I felt better just saying it out loud to her.

Nana looked at me for a minute and I was sure she would think I was feeling sorry for myself, but then she said slowly and thoughtfully. "Well Jeremy, as your Nana, I think we need to work hard together to find some things to help perk you up." And, she began the task immediately by going to her cupboard and taking down a large wooden box from the highest shelf, dusting the top as she sat it on the table.

"Jeremy, when I feel a little down, I find that doing something for someone else always cheers me up."

This wasn't what I wanted to hear. What was she thinking?

"You know, Jeremy, your mother's birthday is next week. I have an idea for something you can make for her that she would like very much." I had forgotten about Mom's birthday; but the prospect of making a gift for her seemed like a good idea and I peered inside the wooden box as Nana opened the lid.

She carefully lifted out several yellowed envelopes filled with black and white photos of people I didn't know. Nana saw my quizzical look and said, "These people are your mom's family, and yours, too," she went on, laying the pictures carefully on the kitchen table. "This is your great uncle Wendall and your great aunt Olena. And here is ..." and she went on, pointing out great grandparents, cousins and more. I wasn't making a connection between this and my mother's birthday. Nana turned to me and said, "Jeremy, this will be your gift to your mom. You and I are going to put all of these photographs in a nice album and make cutouts and paste dried flowers all around them for her. She will be so surprised and pleased!"

I had to admit, it was a good idea and since there was not much else to do, we began that day by drawing different shapes on colored paper and carefully cutting them out to be pasted in the album. As we worked, Nana began telling stories about some of the people in the photographs.

"Now this old gentleman here – he was your great great uncle and came here from Ireland. He was a watchmaker, and I still have one of the watches he made in my drawer upstairs. And he married this lady here (pointing to a grim looking woman with round wire spectacles holding a small child with a giant bow in her hair) – who was once a cook for President Roosevelt."

She went on, working through all of the photos as we cut and pasted, framing each one with cut-out leaves and dried flowers from Nana's summer garden. I had to admit it was interesting, especially when she pointed out my third cousin Claude, wearing a tall hat and boots with spurs, who was a real cowboy and had driven a stagecoach out west.

At one point, we came to a photo of my grandpa, and Nana's eyes misted over as she placed it in the album with a careful, tender touch. "I wish you had known him better," she said wistfully. "I remember our last Christmas together ..." she began, but her words trailed off as she stood up and said, "How about some hot cocoa?" and headed for the stove. A few minutes later I was sipping cocoa topped with melting marshmallows and watching autumn rain patter against the windows. I wondered how long it would be until the first snow fell, since I had never seen snow before and could only imagine what it would be like.

We finished our project in time for mom's birthday, and just like Nana had said, Mom was very surprised, and gave me a major hug when she opened the package. I felt the best I had in a long time and realized that Nana was right about doing something for someone else; it does make you feel happy. She kept me very busy in those days, but still, I sometimes thought about the small door I had seen behind the mop and broom. Nana didn't seem to want me in the pantry, but I decided that it couldn't do any harm if I went in by myself one day when she was busy, just to see what was behind the door.

Over the next few days, Nana had many other projects for us. We baked three pies together all in one day. I learned to help roll out the buttery crusts, while she poured in the hot, fruity fillings.

When we were done we bundled up, climbed in Nana's old blue pickup and took the pies down the road to a few neighbors. At the last house – the closest to our own – the door was opened by a boy about my size. I thought, "Yes! Someone to play with, not too far away." Then another boy appeared who looked exactly like the first. "Twins!" I said out loud.

The boys smiled back and said, "You have twin sisters, too. Our mom told us that."

We were invited in by their mom, and as we sat by a toasty fireplace together, I asked why I hadn't seen them at school. "Well," their mother began. "Both of the boys have spent some time in the hospital recently, but they are better now and will be back at school after Christmas." Their names were Marty and Brian, and they had a collection of Matchbox cars that was the best I had ever seen.

We stayed for almost an hour, and when we left, I was smiling and felt warm inside, even in the chilly winter air. I told Nana, who said, "Well, I *thought* there were some young boys living here, but I hadn't had a chance to visit since they moved in. Perhaps we can play together soon." Things seemed to be looking up. That is, they were until I walked in the door of our cabin.

CHAPTER 4

Lost Friend

Mom and Dad turned when I walked in, and I could see Mom had been crying. "What's wrong?" I asked immediately, wondering what had happened to cause her tears.

"Jeremy, I want you to be strong, and be a big boy" she began – not a good sign. My dad cleared his throat. "Son, we got a call from your aunt Carol, and … well … right after we left, Deano apparently tried to follow us. Carol chased after him, but he wouldn't stop. She put up posters all over and waited to tell us until now, thinking he would come back. But it's been several weeks, and … well … we don't think he'll be found. Deano is gone."

My knees felt weak, and I slumped into a nearby chair. I felt my stomach tightening as I said, "We have to go back and look, Dad. Maybe he's still out there looking for *us*. Please dad, we have to—"

Mom interrupted me. "Jeremy, you have to accept the fact that he's gone. He was a good dog, and we cared about him too. Maybe next spring we can get another dog and ..." she was still talking, but I wasn't hearing anything. Deano had been my dog since he was a tiny ball of blonde fluff. I had taught him tricks, and he would sleep at the foot of my bed and lick my chin every morning to wake me up.

"I don't want another dog; I want *Deano*!" I found myself shouting as I ran to my room and began crying. I skipped dinner that night and tried to understand how this have could happened. I *knew* we shouldn't have left him alone. Part of me blamed Mom and Dad for this whole dumb move anyway, and at first, I could barely talk to them. But after a day or two, I realized it was no one's fault, and I tried hard to accept what had happened. But, I had an ache that not even Nana's special pies and projects could take away.

At school, we began to plan a class Christmas party, but I found it a little hard to get excited along with the other kids. They were beginning to talk to me more though, and that was a good thing. At home, Mom put up a small pine Christmas tree Dad and I had cut down together in the woods by the creek. There were only a few decorations: strings of popcorn, dried cranberries and one string of multi-colored lights. Mom also hinted that with Dad starting a new job and all, there might not be many presents under the tree this year. I said I understood, but it was hard to hear. There were a few special things I had really wanted; a new baseball glove, and a train set; but I could see they would have to wait.

CHAPTER 5

My First Snowfall

The next weekend - the weekend before Christmas - Mom and Dad told me they had to attend the wedding of an old friend in Portland, and that they would take the twins with them, but I would stay with Nana. I was glad and looked forward to spending time with her. I knew that when I came over it brightened her day, and I always felt better, too. I packed up a few things and Mom and Dad dropped me off as they headed on down the road with my sisters both sound asleep in the back seat.

I saw that Nana had put up a small Christmas tree, too. It was complete with some tinsel and silver and blue balls that reflected the light from the candles she had in her windows. That first night we sat on the floor and played "Monopoly" and "Clue" and "Rook". I beat her at each game – but since she was always so focused on making me happy, I wondered if all my "wins" were real.

Nana was so jolly and so much fun. She wasn't really a "regular" grandma. As she kissed me and sent me up to bed, I realized how very close I felt to her, and was ashamed for thinking of myself so much lately. But still, I had a kind of emptiness I couldn't really describe.

The next morning, the house felt especially chilly as Nana woke me with a kiss and said, "Jeremy, take a look outside."

I ran to the window and was amazed at what I saw. The brown, dull ground and grey trees outside had been transformed into a sparkling white wonderland, as large pillowy snowflakes fell and gathered on the ground, the roof of the red barn, and as far as I could see.

"Nana, can we eat breakfast later? I want to go outside," I panted as I pulled on my jeans and red plaid jacket.

Nana laughed at my enthusiasm. "Of course you can," she said, handing me a pair of old rubber boots, a knit cap, and some brown leather gloves. "You'll want these on for sure. It's very cold outside," she said, pulling the cap over my head, and helping me into boots that were way too large, and "clumped" as I ran down the hallway.

She stepped out onto the covered porch with me as I ran down the steps and promptly skidded and fell, laughing as I did, with a soft pillow of snow under me. "This is so great!" I shouted, rolling over and over, licking the snow off my lips as I felt it hitting my face like the gentle touch of many icy fingertips.

Nana smiled and went into the house. "You stay where I can see you now," she cautioned, shutting the big oak door.

I spent the next hour running and sliding, just taking in the unexplainable frosty world I was now a part of. Before long, I heard a noise out back near the barn! When I ran to see, there was my Nana, bundled up in a thick quilted coat, boots, a hat and gloves. She was even plumper with all her padding, and looked like a brightly colored snowman, as she pulled an old wooden sled behind her. "I think this first snowfall calls for a special celebration!" she exclaimed. Nana proceeded to place me on the sled and pull me towards a small hill near the house.

When we reached the top, the hill didn't look small anymore and I began to feel a little concerned. "Jeremy, you are about to take your first sled ride, and I am going with you." I couldn't believe it, but sure enough, Nana gave us a little push, climbed gingerly on the sled behind me, and before I knew it, we were headed down the hill. I was laughing hard, partly to hide my fear as the cold wind hit my cheeks and the snow flew up in front of us, so we could barely see.

"Pull the cord to the right!" Nana shouted in my ear, and I did, but not before we slid off course and plowed into an old pile of grass clippings covered with snow at the bottom of the hill. We both rolled off, and lay there laughing until Nana said, "Well, we might as well make snow angels while we're down here." And she began waving her arms and legs out to the side in a very un-grandmotherly way. After a few trips down the hill together, she headed into the house and left me on my own to master the art of steering a sled downhill.

An hour later, I was called into the house to warm up with a cheese sandwich grilled in real butter on top of the old cook stove, and hot cider stirred with a stick of real cinnamon. My fingers and the tip of my nose felt numb, but I remember giggling throughout the entire meal. As I finished, Nana bundled up again and said, "Now, your first snowman."

She proceeded to lead me outside where we rolled a giant ball of snow, topped by another a little bit smaller, and then another, about the size of a choice Halloween pumpkin. Soon, rock "eyes" were in place and a bent carrot became a nose. An old striped flannel blanket was wrapped around his shoulders, and fuzzy earmuffs topped it off.

"You're on your own now, Jeremy. I'm cold, and have some important things to do inside. I'll call you in a little while, but come in if you get too chilly," she said, waving from the front porch.

I lost track of time as I built my first snow fort and had imaginary battles with cowboys and Indians, mastering the art of throwing an accurate snowball at invisible enemies. It was getting close to dark, as I regrettably gave in to the command from Nana to come in and walked onto the porch where we brushed frozen chunks of snow from my pants and shoes.

CHAPTER 6

A Secret Shared

Later that evening by the fire, I said, "Nana, this was my best day since I've been here". She smiled back, stroking my hair as we worked on a puzzle together.

"So … are you feeling better now?" she asked, concern in her soft voice.

"Yes," I sighed. "But I still miss Deano and at night, I still have that kind of empty feeling where my belly is," I said honestly.

Nana was silent for a minute before she said, "Jeremy, I have been deciding whether or not to show you something very special to me. But if I do, you must keep it a secret."

My heart skipped as I looked at her face in the firelight. Surely, this was something important and I nodded eagerly, "Yes, Nana, of course." She looked right into my eyes, seeming to search for something, and then to find it there.

"All right," she said softly. "Come with me." She took my hand as we walked back towards the kitchen. I looked out through the candle-lit windows and could see that an inky darkness had settled in outside. She went straight to the door of the pantry and opened it slowly and deliberately.

"Jeremy, before we go in, I want to tell you something. Your grandpa was the love of my life. I don't expect you to understand that now, but one day you will. He and I had so many special times together. And our favorite day each year was Christmas. This house would be *filled* with company during the holidays, and it was such a happy time. We were always so sad when Christmas was over. So your grandpa decided he wanted a special place, just for us – just him and me - where we could have the wonderful feelings Christmas brings, *anytime we wanted to.* Even in the summer. So he fixed this place for me, where it would be Christmas year 'round, just so we could always have that special feeling that only comes to most people once a year, and … so … well … I'll just show you."

By then I felt as though I had stopped breathing. She took my hand as we walked past the fruit and butter to the back of the pantry where she moved aside the old mop and bucket. And yes, just as I had thought, there was another door there. Nana took my hand again as she opened it, and we began going down a narrow wooden staircase, lit only by one light bulb, hanging from a single wire. Cobwebs hung on the walls, and the thought of giant spiders crossed my mind for a quick moment. When we reached the bottom, there was another small door.

Nana's voice became very quiet as she said, "Merry Christmas, Jeremy," and opened the last door to reveal an amazing, magical sight.

We were in a very large room, with tall windows looking out over the dark valley of pine trees below the house. But what was in the room? It was unbelievable! In the far corner was a giant silvery Christmas tree, lit with strings of bubble lights and tiny painted lampshades that twirled on soft blue bulbs, creating dancing lights and pictures on the ceiling and walls. Tinsel on the tree reflected the light even more and it was as though the whole room was sparkling and moving. Lights around the windows reflected even more twinkling images into the room, adding to the feeling of movement. Flickering candles were scattered around the room, and dozens of boxes wrapped in cheery paper and bright red bows were under the tree. Christmas carols played softly on an old record player, and a warm fire crackled in a fireplace in the corner where red stockings hung on the mantle with the names "Irene" and "Ben–my nana and papa–" embroidered on their white furry tops.

We slowly walked further into the room. Hand-made wooden toys of all kinds were scattered around. I saw bowls of hard-candy on a table between two rocking chairs, along with an old cherry-wood pipe, and I looked up to see a large silver star on top of the tree which was also adorned with gauzy, wispy angels with glittering wings, as well as candy canes and golden tinsel.

I felt as though I had walked into a dream, and realized I had not said a word since we opened the door. "Nana," I whispered, because whispering seemed appropriate in this room. "Nana, what is this place?"

"This is my secret Christmas room, Jeremy," she said, and looked around as though she, too, were seeing it for the first time. I waited for her to go on.

"You see," she said, in a soft voice. "Your Grandpa made me promise I would *never* lose what we called our special "Christmas feeling" even after … he was gone. So, I have kept this room, just as we created it together, and filled it with our special memories. I don't ever take the decorations down, in summer, fall or spring. And when I feel lonely, I come here and turn on the lights, and hum our familiar carols, and it's almost like we are together again, though I know that can't be. But that *feeling* that only comes to most people at Christmas? Well, it comes to me every time I'm here and it keeps me happy year-round."

My ten-year-old heart could hardly take it all in. This incredible room and the love that made it happen.

Nana saw me looking at some of the toys scattered around the room and said "Jeremy, it's okay to play here. Your grandpa had always hoped you would be able to come here for a long visit, and he is the one who carved and painted all the wooden toys you see, so this room will be yours now, too. But no one else knows. I just can't do that right now."

I think I understood what it took for her to finally open this part of her life to me, and I would have given up anything I had before I would betray her confidence in me.

Nana walked over and picked up a book of Christmas stories, and asked if I would like her to read to me. She gathered some of the wooden toy soldiers, and I climbed on her lap in the rocking chair, which creaked a comforting sound as she rocked back and forth. I listened to the stories while I admired the incredible carved soldiers, made for me, by a grandpa I hadn't known. I could see his delicate brush strokes in the red painted cheeks and bright jackets of the toys I held.

I didn't want the night or the feeling to end. When Nana said we had to go upstairs and get ready for bed, my heart sank. "Jeremy, you and I will come here every weekend when you stay with me. This will be our secret, and we'll read and play, and bring our little projects here. It will be Christmas every day in this room. But remember, part of Christmas is prayer, talking to God, and asking for miracles for others. And we will do that here, too."

And one day, I knelt in our Christmas Room and silently asked God for a miracle for me, not really believing that it could ever come true.

CHAPTER 7

The Best Day Ever

The very next weekend, we once again slipped down to our secret room, where we danced silly dances to cheery Christmas carols and together, read some of the old books she and grandpa had collected. Nana had baked buttery cookies and we brought them downstairs and decorated them with creamy frosting and red and green sprinkles and munched away, until an entire dozen was gone. We made fudge, then peppermint sticks another night and worked for hours on our special Christmas projects for Mom and Dad and the girls.

On one especially magical night, we turned off all the lights except the ones on the tree and lay on the carpet on a pile of old pillows embroidered with snowmen, and looked out the tall windows at the wintry sky. The moon was full and it was so cold and crisp outside, it looked as though we could see a million stars in the black winter sky. Moonlight reflecting on the snow made the ground look like it was sprinkled with tiny diamonds. A sudden movement just outside the window made me sit up quickly to see three deer in the yard, looking in our direction.

"Shhhh" Nana whispered, as she reached for a small burlap sack by the fireplace. Opening it, she scooped out a small tin of grain pellets, and handed some to me. Then she quietly opened the tall sliding window that went nearly to the floor and wagged her finger for me to follow her as she carefully climbed outside.

"Come here my babies," she said ever so softly, walking through the snow towards the deer, holding her woolen sweater tightly around her. I followed, and watched as the deer hesitantly came towards her, then I stood frozen in time as first one, then the other two, gently ate the grain from her hands, moonlight reflected in their dark eyes.

"Jeremy, hold out your hand" she whispered, and I did – only to have the smallest deer come towards me, watching my face as it silently approached. Then I felt its soft warm tongue, as it took the grain from my shaking hands, stepping back when the pellets were gone, then joined the other two deer as they slipped back into the darkness of the surrounding trees.

"They are a family and have been coming here for a few years," Nana said. "Your grandpa and I used to feed them too. Now, you will be their new friend." We crept back into the house, very cold, but warmed by the beauty of the gentle visitors.

Christmas was just two days later, and it was very nice, as we all gathered at our cabin to feast on a large browned turkey, and opened our small pile of gifts from under the tree. Mom, Dad and the girls really liked the things Nana and I had made for them, and somehow, Dad and Mom had managed to buy the baseball mitt and train I had wanted. We snacked on more turkey, talked and laughed and then had puffy lemon meringue pie. It seemed like we ate for hours!

A few days later, I heard the twin boys we had met were feeling much better, planned to start school in a few days, and would be riding the bus with me now. Feeling happy was something I had almost forgotten about, but my time with Nana in our Christmas room was helping me to feel very thankful for what I *did* have. But, there was another great thing left to happen.

I was outside playing in the front yard of our cabin working on a tall snowman when Dad pulled swiftly into the yard in the station wagon, nearly clipping the corner of the garage. He had been on a short trip along the Oregon coast to bring back a new piece of equipment needed at the mill, and at first, I thought he was just glad to be home. But when I ran towards the car and saw his face, I knew there was something else going on. He jumped out, put his hands on my shoulders and said, "Jeremy, I know you're not going to believe this. I can't believe it myself, but when I was driving along the coast—" He was interrupted by a loud bark from the back of the car.

"*Deano,*" I screamed as my long-lost best friend jumped out of the window and began covering me in sloppy dog kisses. "Deano, my dog, my friend, my very own dog," I cried over and over, hugging him, feeling his soft fur against my face as I held his head in my arms. He was plenty dirty and looked thin, but he was home.

We ran to the house to show Mom and the girls, but I couldn't wait to take Deano up to Nana's. When she saw him and heard the story, she cried with me as we petted and stroked him and held him close. I stopped for a minute and looked over at her. "Nana," I bent over and whispered in her ear "*This* was my prayer. This was the miracle I prayed for in our Christmas room. Deano – back with me." Nana smiled and hugged me as we shared the joy of our secret time together. I will treasure that moment as long as I live; nothing will ever compare.

CHAPTER 8

We Will Stay

D ad and Mom decided after a few years in Oregon that we would not go back to California. I had made many good friends here; the girls would soon start kindergarten, and the mill was doing better than expected.

For many years, our good times continued. The secret Nana and I shared was kept, and so much good, so many gifts and cards for others, prayers for the hurting, along with a lot of laughter and joy came from that room. And every time I went to see her, and we opened the secret door in the pantry - spring, summer or fall - that same wonderful feeling I felt the very first time - the Christmas Feeling - always returned.

Just as I entered my teens, my precious Nana became ill during the winter. Her heart just grew tired, and after spending a few days at the hospital with dad by her side, he returned home one day with a look that I knew could only mean, my Nana was gone. The old empty feeling threatened to overtake me again.

A few days later, Mom was going through some of Nana's things and found a note written by Nana, addressed to me, about the time she first got sick. It read, "My special, wonderful Jeremy: If I don't get well, please don't be sad. I want you to remember our special Christmas feeling and I want you to know this all just means that my *own* miracle came true." Mom asked if I knew what that meant, and I couldn't answer out loud, but I did know. The miracle Nana asked for in our Christmas Room had come to be. She was home with Grandpa again.

Later that year, we all moved into Nana's house, which she had wanted us to have. It was almost a year before I showed my parents the secret room, because at first, I wasn't ready. I had learned from Nana that love runs deep, and it takes time to get to a place where you can speak about its loss. At a time when I had thought my ten-year-old heart could never feel happy again, my "Nana" had been sent into my life to help me through. The incredible memories, and her kind, giving spirit and example are still with me today, and have shaped who I am and how I live. And that truly is a miracle. I miss you Nana. Merry Christmas today, every day and always.

Milton Keynes UK
Ingram Content Group UK Ltd.
UKHW052157071124
450767UK00005B/20

9 781965 679272